Dragon Tales

ZAK AND WHEEZIE CLEAN UP

I wish, I wish
With all my heart
To fly with dragons
In a land apart.

By Irene Trimble
Based on a story by Cliff Ruby & Elana Lesser
Illustrated by The Thompson Brothers
Based on the characters by Ron Rodecker

Visit Dragon Tales on the Web at www.dragontales.com
Watch us on PBS!

Max was digging through his giant toy box one bright afternoon.

"Look, I found my favorite drum!" Max called to his big sister, Emmy. "Have you seen my drumsticks?"

"Gee, Max," Emmy mumbled,
staring at her feet. "I thought
those old drumsticks were just
garbage. So I...threw them away."
"You threw them away?!"
cried Max.

Max couldn't believe what Emmy had done to his drumsticks. After all, anyone could tell that his beautiful sticks were *not* garbage. But before he could say anything, the magic dragon scale in their playroom began to shimmer and glow.

"Look, Emmy!" Max cried. "The dragons are calling us!"

"We'll look for the drumsticks later," Emmy promised her brother as she picked up the glowing dragon scale.

And just as it always did, the magic scale took them on a fantastic journey to a wonderful place called Dragon Land!

Max and Emmy landed right beside a deep tunnel called a knuckerhole.

"Come on!" cried Emmy as she jumped in. "This is the way to Zak and Wheezie's cave!"

Max quickly followed. And soon the children were sliding up, down, and all around the corkscrew curves of the crazy knuckerhole.

Max and Emmy tumbled out at the feet of their favorite two-headed dragon.

"Hi, Zak! Hi, Wheezie!" said Max. The children watched as Zak dumped a basketful of tinfoil and string into a garbage chute.

"You're just in time," said Wheezie, whose eyes were shut tight. "Zakky has a big surprise for me, but I can't peek until he's all finished."

Zak leaned over and whispered to Max and Emmy, "I'm cleaning Wheezie's side of the cave so it will be nice and neat, just like mine. She's going to be so surprised!"

"Uh-oh!" thought Emmy, remembering Max's drumsticks. Before she could warn Zak, he dumped the last of Wheezie's things down the deep, dark garbage chute.

"Okay, Wheezie," said Zak. "Open your eyes for the big surprise!"

Wheezie opened her eyes—and almost spit fire when she looked at her empty side of the cave.
"Where's my favorite ball of tinfoil? And my slippery green rock collection? And my best button bracelet?" she asked.
"*Where are all my things?!*"

"What do you mean?" answered Zak. He couldn't understand why Wheezie seemed so upset. "All I did was throw away the trash."

"You threw away all my beautiful treasures, Zakky!" cried Wheezie as she rushed to look down the garbage chute. "We have to go down to the garbage cave and find them!"

"Not that garbage cave!" groaned Zak as Wheezie dragged him along.

It was too late! The dark garbage cave was empty.

"All my treasures are gone," Wheezie said, sniffling. "Arlo the garbage dragon has already taken everything away to the Dragon Dump."

"We could fly to the Dragon Dump and find your things," Zak suggested with a sigh. Zak hated the thought of all that smelly trash. But he really wanted to make things up to his sister Wheezie.

Wheezie was delighted! So Max and Emmy held on tight as the dragons took to the sky.

"Wow," said Max as they flew over the giant mountain of trash. "There must be a gazillion tons of garbage down there."

"Yup. And a giant recycling machine, too," Wheezie added.

The dragons and their friends came in for a landing right in the middle of the Dragon Dump. They found Arlo the garbage dragon stuffing piles of trash into a big machine.

"I'm sorry, Wheezie," Arlo said when he heard about their mission. "The garbage from your cave has already gone into my old recycler here."

"In here?" asked Wheezie as she leaned over to peer deep into the giant recycling machine.

"Wheezie!" yelled Zak. "Don't lean that far!" But it was too late. Wheezie lost her footing and fell right into the machine! And she pulled Zak, Emmy, and Max in with her!

"Oh, yuck!" whined Zak as everyone landed in a huge pile of garbage.
"Look!" called Wheezie. "Here's my yellow yarn! And my favorite tinfoil
ball! And my slippery green rock collection!" She hugged her treasures close.
"Does this mean we can go home now?" asked Zak.

"Not until we find my button bracelet,"
Wheezie answered.

After they had searched for a while, all they had found was one shiny purple button. "My button bracelet just isn't here," sobbed Wheezie.

"Guess it's gone, just like my drumsticks," said Max.

"I'm sorry, Max," Emmy told her brother. "I'll never throw away anything that's yours again."

"I'm sorry, too," Zak told Wheezie. "I'll make you another bracelet. I promise!"

"Did you find all your buried treasures, Wheezie?" Arlo asked as the friends climbed out of his recycling machine.

"Not everything," Wheezie said with a sigh. "But Zak found a pretty purple button for me."

"That button sure would look fine on this," Arlo said as he jingled a bracelet on his arm.

Wheezie's eyes lit up and her little dragon heart soared. "Look!" she cried. "It's my button bracelet, safe and sound!"

"Well, bust my britches!" said Arlo as he carefully tied the bracelet around Wheezie's wrist. "I knew this bracelet was too good to be trash!"

Wheezie thanked Arlo with a big dragon kiss. But before waving good-bye, she handed him the purple button.

"So you can start your own button bracelet," Wheezie explained.

Soon Zak and Wheezie
were soaring back to their
dragon cave, and Emmy and
Max were taking their own
magical journey back home.

"Now let's see about those drumsticks," Emmy said to Max. She emptied the trash can onto the floor of their playroom.

"*There* they are!" Max shouted. He grabbed his drumsticks and began to beat on his drum. Max was banging so loud, Emmy could barely hear him say, "Thanks, Emmy!"